**Library of Congress Cataloging in Publication Data**

Hefter, Richard.
  Hippo jogs for health.

  (Sweet Pickles series ; 15)
  SUMMARY : The Sweet Pickles ambassador for
good health doesn't know when to stop jogging.
  [1. Hippopotamus—Fiction] I. Title.
II. Series.
PZ7.H3587Hi          [E]          77-16320
ISBN 0-03-042026-1

# THIS

## SWEET PICKLES ™

## BOOK BELONGS TO

Kurt Smith

In the world of *Sweet Pickles*, each
animal gets into a pickle because of an
all too human personality trait.

This book is about Healthy Hippo who
always has the latest and greatest
answer for keeping fit. This week it's jogging.

Books in the Sweet Pickles Series:

# HIPPO
# JOGS
# FOR HEALTH

Written and Illustrated by
Richard Hefter

Edited by Ruth Lerner Perle

**Holt, Rinehart and Winston · New York**

"Hup, huff. Hup, huff," panted Hippo as he jogged past
Goose's house very early in the morning.
Goose was sleeping in her hammock.
She opened one eye.

"You're up early," said Hippo.
Goose opened the other eye. "What?" she yawned.
"Early? It's not early. It's only evening and I haven't
had my supper yet."

"Silly Goose," smiled Hippo. "You must have fallen asleep here last night because it's very early in the morning now."

"Oh, dear," sighed Goose. "If it's morning, I suppose I should think about eating breakfast pretty soon."

"Quite right," smiled Hippo. "But there's nothing healthier than a fast jog before breakfast."

"A what?" yawned Goose.

"A good bracing jog," laughed Hippo. "A healthy run, a nice stiff trot. There's nothing like it for a healthy body and a healthy mind. See, it says so right here in this booklet."

"What's that?" yawned Goose again.

*"JOGGING FOR HEALTH!"* said Hippo proudly. "It's the latest selection from my Health Book of the Week Club. Here's one for you." Hippo handed Goose a little book.

"Is that anything like the *CARROT JUICE FOR HEALTH* book you gave me last week?" asked Goose. "Carrot juice is OK," said Hippo, "but jogging is *really* healthy for you."

"But when you gave me the carrot juice book, you told me *that* was really healthy for you," said Goose. "And before that you gave me a book on HEADSTANDS FOR HEALTH and before that it was YOGURT AND YOGA, and before that it was..."

"Yes, yes," snorted Hippo. "But this is the latest thing. This is JOGGING. And jogging is the real answer. Come jog with me and I'll make a new Goose out of you."

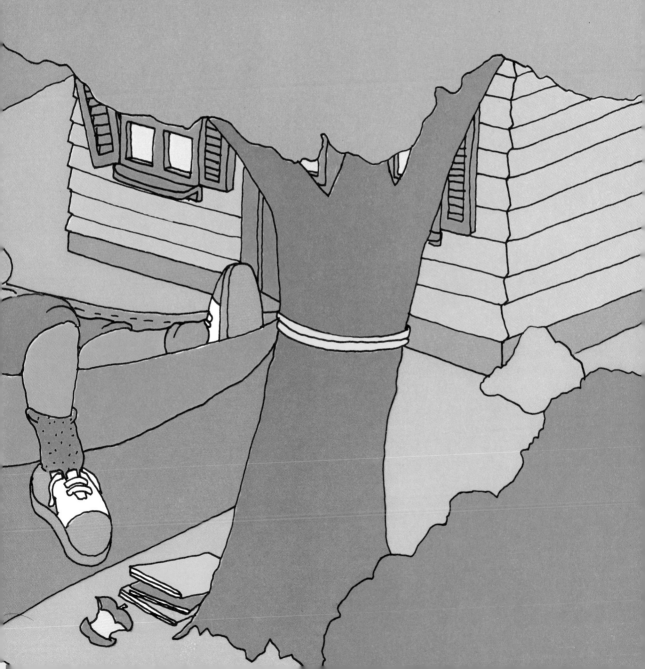

"I'd like to," sighed Goose, "but I'm still thinking about the yogurt and yoga. And besides, it's almost time for breakfast. Maybe I'll come along tomorrow."

Hippo started to run in place. "Hup, huff. Hup, huff."

"Tomorrow," mumbled Goose and she rolled over and went back to sleep.

"Hup, huff. Hup, huff." Hippo jogged off.

Rabbit was hanging the wash as Hippo came by. "Good morning, Rabbit," shouted Hippo. "How about joining me for a nice healthy jog?"

"No time for jogging," said Rabbit, looking at his watch. "Too much to do. Have to stay on schedule."

"You should fit jogging into your schedule," puffed Hippo. "Jogging gives you a healthy body and a healthy mind. Here, read this." Hippo tossed a booklet to Rabbit.

"I'll read it next Wednesday evening," said Rabbit. "I'm busy until then."

"Hup, huff," said Hippo. "That's a long time to wait for a healthy body and a healthy mind."

Hippo turned around and jogged on. He passed Elephant's house. "Hey, Elephant," he shouted. "Want to come for a jog? It's really healthy for you!"

"No, thanks," smiled Elephant. "But you look tired. Why don't you stop and have some breakfast with me?"

"I can't stop," snorted Hippo. "Jogging is the latest and the greatest. Here, read this."

Hippo jogged up Fourth Street and down Main Street. He jogged across the bridge over the water. He jogged around the dump and over the Old Bridge and up to Park Avenue.

"Huff, huff," he puffed. "This sure is healthy."

Hippo jogged around the Medical Center and past the Tower Apartments.

"Puff, puff," he huffed. "Everybody should do this."

Hippo passed Camel.

"Look out!" she shouted. "Wet cement!"
Hippo jumped out of the way.
"Hey there, Camel," he panted. "How about a healthy jog?"

Camel looked up at Hippo. His face looked hot. His eyes were bulging. He could hardly catch his breath. "You don't look so healthy," said Camel.

"But jogging is, puff, puff, very healthy!" gasped Hippo. "And I've been jogging for three and a half hours!"

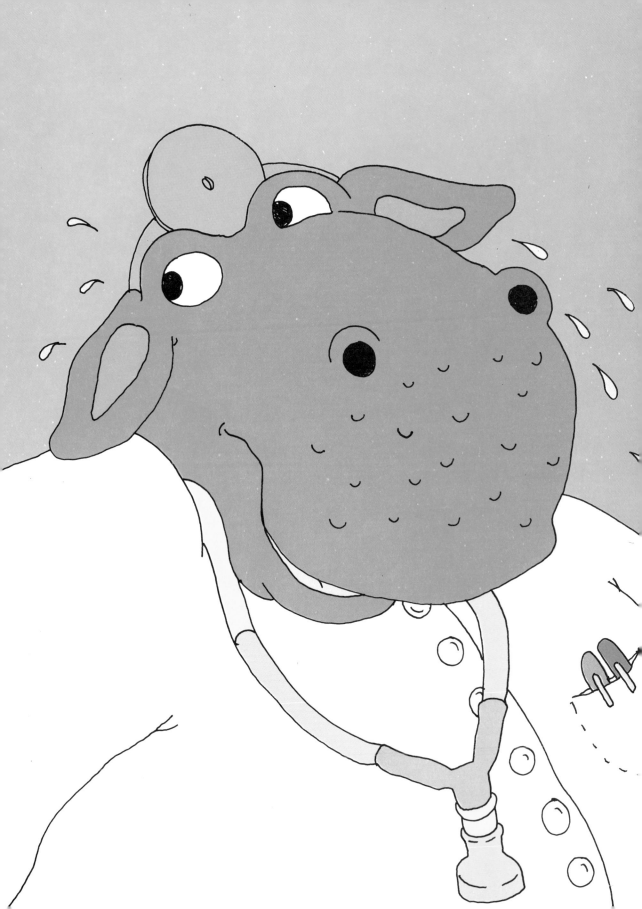

"I think it would be healthier," warned Camel, "to stop for now. You never know when to stop. Last week, you almost drowned in a tub of carrot juice. Before that, it took a crane to stop your two-day-headstand. And before that..."

"But, Camel," interrupted Hippo. "Jogging builds a healthy body and a healthy mind. It's the latest and the greatest." He huffed and puffed and kept on jogging.

He jogged up Fifth Street.
He jogged across Main Street.
He jogged down Center Street and back onto Park Avenue.

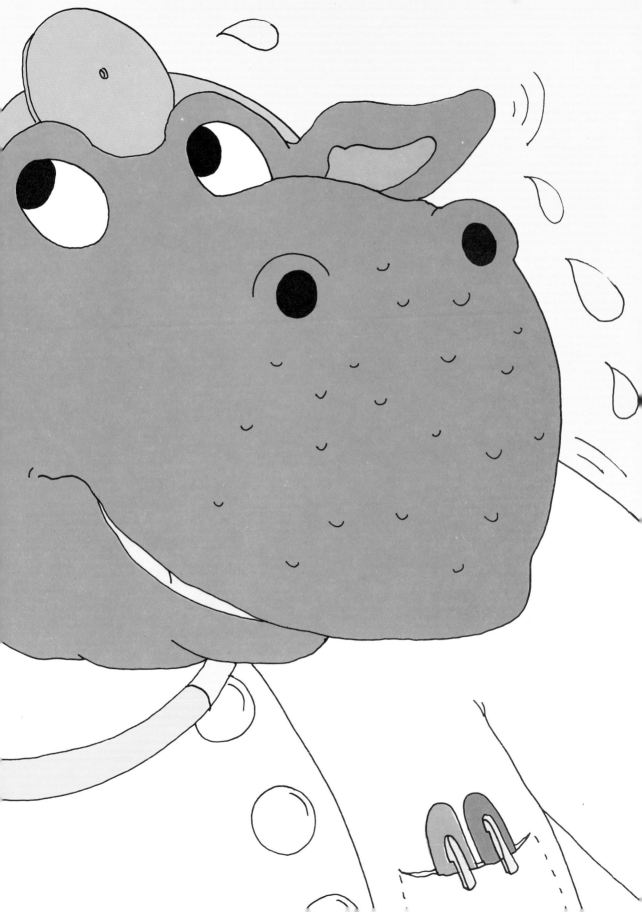

"Huff, huff, puff," gasped Hippo.
"Puff, huff.
"Huff!
"Puff!
"Pfft!"

Hippo sank down on the sidewalk and collapsed.
Everyone rushed over.
"You look sick!" shouted Rabbit.

"Sick! Oh, no!" groaned Hippo. "I've never been healthier. I've been jogging. Jogging builds a healthy body…HUFF…and a healthy mind…PUFF…! It says so right here in this book!"

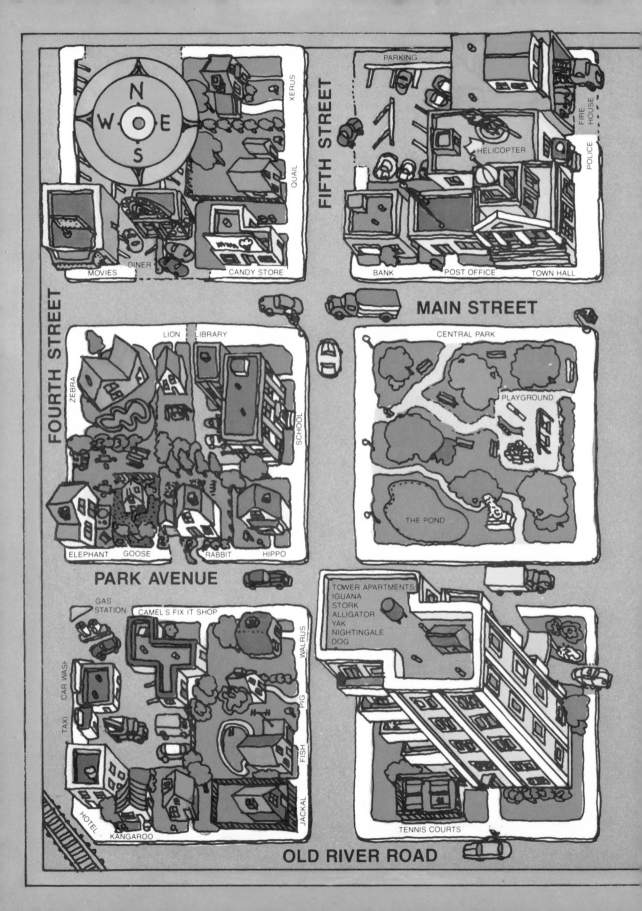